# HEADCASE

# BAD COFFEE AND WORSE LUCK

## KEN MACGREGOR
## &
## KERRY LIPP

PUBLICATIONS

Lycan Valley Press Publications
1625 E 72nd St STE 700 PMB 132
Tacoma, Washington 98404 United States of America

Printed in the United States of America

First Serialized Edition, August 2020

ISBN-13: 978-1-64562-974-0

*For Liz*

# CHAPTER 1

Johnny Headcase sat across the Formica counter from the punk kid with blue hair and a white, stained apron. A gauze bandage clung to the kid's neck. *Bloodsucker bait,* Johnny thought.

"You let vampires feed on you, right?"

"What? No." A sheen of sweat broke out on the kid's forehead.

Johnny met his gaze and held it. A stainless steel ring twitched in the kid's lip as he turned away. After a moment, he turned back with a glass urn. The guy's gaze traveled over Johnny's scarred face, but wouldn't meet his eyes.

The kid poured Johnny's coffee into a chipped mug with a shaky hand and a clenched jaw.

"Anyway, I don't have to tell you shit," he said.

He was dripping sweat now, standing on the other side of the counter. The air conditioner was going full blast and it hovered around seventy degrees in the diner. The punk's blue mohawk quivered and his fingers tapped nonstop against his thigh.

Johnny nodded, pursed his lips and said nothing.

The kid sneered at Johnny, but there was fear in the boy's eyes.

Johnny sipped his coffee. He frowned at it.

"This coffee is terrible. You should be ashamed of yourself, serving this to people."

"Whatever, man," the kid said. "Why are you hassling me?"

Johnny swirled the coffee around in his cup and took another sip. It hadn't gotten any better. He looked up and caught the kid's eye.

After several silent seconds, the kid took a deep breath, then let it out. His shoulders sagged.

"Look, man. I swear I don't know anything. They always meet me somewhere different, you know?"

Johnny nodded again, swallowed more horrid coffee, and stood up. The kid's head tilted, angled almost straight up to look Johnny in the eyes. The only other customer in the diner developed a sudden and profound interest in his menu.

Johnny inhaled deeply and let it out of his nose in a rush.

"I'm going to give you twenty dollars. If you don't tell me where I can find the vampires, I'm going to give you another twenty."

The kid blinked.

"Wait. What?"

Johnny pulled his hands from his pockets. He

showed the kid the roll of quarters in each hand, wrapped his fists around them and hit the kid in the face twice.

The second punch came with a crunch.

"Shit! You broke my nose!"

"Tell me where they are."

"I don't know." The kid touched his nose. "Jesus, that hurts."

Johnny gave the kid another twenty bucks.

The punk spat out a tooth. The words followed it.

"Elysium Fields Cemetery. The big crypt by the back fence."

"Thank you," Johnny said.

He had been so helpful, Johnny gave him an extra ten. The kid hit the floor, unconscious.

On the way out, Johnny Headcase caught the eye of the man in the booth by the door, the one with the fascinating menu.

"Don't order the coffee," Johnny said. "It'll only piss you off."

# CHAPTER 2

JOHNNY WALKED out of the diner with a bad taste in his mouth, and it came from more than just the coffee. He'd finally found the vampires, as long as the blue-haired freak had spoken the truth. Johnny learned a long time ago when someone had that much blood pouring out of a crooked nose, honesty tended to flow after it.

He could also count on the punk tipping them off. They'd probably be expecting Johnny Headcase. Might be better to think this through than to go in guns blazing. He preferred running and gunning but he also preferred not dying. Or worse, dying and coming back.

Dusk highlighted the horizon like a fresh bruise, and he wasn't about to tackle a flock of vampires after dark. He was reckless at times, sure, but never stupid.

The taste of the foul coffee sat on his tongue like a dead rat, but the caffeine gave him false vigor to go with his real attitude. He walked faster as thoughts of this latest threat to his town throttled his head. Pinching the bridge of his nose, Johnny grumbled.

"God damn it. I hate vampires."

Wandering through one of the seedier sections of King City, he burned off some of his energy unconsciously looking for an inevitable fight. When he found one, he'd burn off the rest.

It didn't take long. Two young punks with weird hair who could've been related to the guy at the diner. The Moron Brothers. They were all up in a homeless guy's grill, badgering him, heaping abuses on him both verbal and physical.

The homeless guy hunched like a bearded dirty twig on two legs. No hope, nor chance of fighting back.

Fate stepped in.

Fate's name was Johnny Headcase.

"Seriously?" Johnny said.

The punks' heads whipped around. They had spiked hair the colors of an aborted rainbow. More metal than skin covered their faces and tattoos covered the rest.

The one with pink and orange hair spat on the ground.

"The fuck do you want?"

"Look at this pathetic waste," Johnny said and pointed to the homeless guy. "Christ, he's got limbs like toothpicks. Probably hasn't eaten anything but garbage all week."

"It's true, I haven't. They was stealing my change," the homeless guy said. His nuts had apparently just dropped.

One of the kids started to open his mouth.

"Don't. Just shut up. Holes in your face, ink on your arms, and kicking the shit out of a homeless guy doesn't scare me and doesn't make you tough."

The other one spat. Apparently, this was how they announced their intent to speak.

"What the hell do you know about being tough?"

Johnny squeezed his eyes shut and pinched the bridge of his nose. It was turning out to be that kind of day.

"More than a pathetic little shit like you will ever learn."

"Better listen up, you freaky queers," the homeless guy said.

Johnny's lip twitched upward, but he managed not to laugh.

"Tell you guys what," Johnny said, reaching into his pockets. "You wanna rob people for change, here's twenty bucks in quarters. All yours. Come and get it." He wrapped his big fists around the rolls of quarters. His knuckles were an atlas of scar tissue.

The two exchanged a glance and backed down.

"Smart choice," Johnny said. "You get to live another day. Now, show me your backs."

Fury and shame warred on their faces as the two walked away. Toward the cemetery, Johnny noticed.

He put the quarters away and stepped over to the homeless guy.

"You all right, tough guy?"

"Yeah. Thanks for that; they come around sometimes. Don't hurt me much but mess my day up all the same."

Johnny nodded.

"They heading toward the cemetery?"

The homeless guy shrugged. "Could be. I know they talk about it sometimes. Name's Snake Eyes." He extended his hand.

Black and gray dirt streaked his skin. Johnny shook it anyway.

"Why do they call you that?"

"Snake Eyes are always bad luck and bad luck always seems to find me. That's why I'm here in these oh-so-delightful digs."

"I'm Johnny Headcase."

The dirt on the man's face cracked as he smiled.

"Where the hell did you get a name like that?"

Johnny grinned.

"You commit one quadruple homicide and people never let you live it down."

Snake Eyes became Huge Eyes.

"You killed four people?"

"That time, yeah. Nice to meet you. Keep your eyes open. Lots of assholes out here."

Snake Eyes put up his fist to be bumped.

"Testify."

Johnny shook his head and tried not to laugh. He

bumped the other man's fist and smiled. He liked this guy. Johnny took a few steps in the direction the freaks had fled.

"Hey mister," Snake Eyes said. He shook a Styrofoam cup. "Can you spare some change?"

"No. But, I can spare a bill."

Johnny pulled out his two rolls of quarters, held them in one hand and fished a dollar bill out of his other pocket. He balled it up and tossed it in the cup from four feet away.

"Whoa," Snake Eyes said. "Nice shot."

"Look after yourself, Snake Eyes," Johnny said.

He waited for a car to pass and crossed the street. On the other side of the wrought iron fence, Johnny could barely make out the name Wilson, Frank above the birth and death dates. The sun was almost gone now and Johnny's survival instincts kicked in.

"Right," he said aloud. "Vampires. Nighttime. Bad idea."

Johnny shook his head. The Moron Brothers would have to wait.

# CHAPTER 3

JOHNNY SAT on the edge of the bed, pulling on his boots. Behind him, Darla turned over and ran her fingers over the scars on Johnny's back. When she moved, he caught a whiff of her perfume. *Cinnabar*, she said it was called. He loved the smell. He glanced at her over his shoulder. She threw him a lazy smile.

"How many times have you been shot?" Darla asked.

"Nine."

"Jesus. Stabbed?"

"Don't know. I lost track," Johnny said with a shrug.

"Is there anybody tougher than you, Johnny Headcase?"

"Not so far," Johnny said, pulling on his shirt. Darla stretched like a cat. Johnny paused in the middle of putting on his shoulder holster to watch her. Darla tossed him a smile full of promise.

"You want to come back to bed, baby?"

"Yeah, but I have work to do," Johnny said.

"Rain check?" Darla asked, raising one knee to give Johnny a good view of what he was turning down. Not for the first time, he wondered why a beauty like her stuck around with a brute like him. Also, he wondered if maybe he wasn't the only one in her life. He wasn't sure how he'd feel about it if that was the case. He hoped he never had to find out.

Johnny nodded, pulled his jacket on over his gun and left Darla's apartment.

He and Darla weren't in a committed relationship. It was more of a frequently horizontal one. But Johnny had come to appreciate her for more than just her talents in the sack. If he was the kind of man to settle down, Darla was the kind of woman Johnny would want to settle with. Pulling the door shut behind him, he wore a rare, wistful smile.

Stepping out into the sunshine, Johnny turned downtown. An ice cream truck crept by playing "Pop Goes the Weasel" over and over. The guy hunched over the steering wheel looked like he'd rather be anywhere else. The faded painting on the side was a clown holding popsicles out. Its grin didn't look happy so much as insane.

The buildings were built close together with garbage cans in the alleys between them. Saplings stood every ten feet by the curb. In the fifteen years

Johnny had lived in this town, the trees hadn't shown much sign of growth. Residential buildings gave way to storefronts with apartments above. Halfway down the second block, Johnny opened the door to Nick's Bakery.

The smell of fresh donuts made Johnny salivate. Nick worked behind the glass counter, wielding a rolling pin with the practiced ease of a master. When he saw Johnny, he grinned.

"It can't be your birthday yet. It's still warm out."

Every year, on November 8th, Johnny came to Nick's and got a jelly donut. It was the one sugary thing he allowed himself and only once a year.

"I'm calling in a favor, Nick," Johnny said.

Nick's grin died and his hands went still, the dough forgotten. He didn't meet the other man's eyes. After several seconds, he sighed and looked up.

"Of course, Johnny. I wouldn't be behind this counter if wasn't for you. Anything you need."

Johnny grinned.

"That slumlord who used to own this building had way too many teeth. I felt obligated to knock a few of 'em out. Besides, your bakery is just what this neighborhood needed. It has gone way uphill since you opened."

"I appreciate it just the same. What's up?"

Johnny told Nick what he needed and the other man swallowed hard but nodded. Johnny left.

At best, Nick wouldn't be ready to help Johnny until morning. Johnny didn't like waiting another day, but patience often paid off. In his younger days he'd taken all kinds of unnecessary risks and had the scars to prove it. He'd mellowed a bit with age. Still every bit as dangerous, but battle-hardened, and he'd rather fight smart than fight hard. But, one way or another, he'd always take the fight.

He licked his lips as he stepped out of the bakery. The low sun brightened the morning of the dingy city and Johnny turned and walked back into Nick's Bakery.

Nick saw him and immediately raised his hands like a bandit cornered by the cops.

"C'mon man, you said that was it," Nick said, eyes bulging.

"Relax, guy," Johnny said. "I just want a cup of coffee."

Nick sighed and sagged. He filled up a large Styrofoam cup of piping hot black coffee.

"You drink this stuff like Jack Reacher," Nick said.

"Yeah, well, I guess that guy is onto something right?" Then he puffed out some air and said, "Reacher's a fucking amateur," under his breath.

"On the house." Nick grinned. "Now get the hell out of here."

"One more thing," Johnny said and reached into his pocket.

Nick gulped.

Johnny pulled out a dollar bill, wadded it up and tossed it into the tip jar. From five feet away.

"I'll take that donut after all."

"Really?"

"Life's short, Nick."

Nick handed Johnny a jelly donut in a tiny paper bag.

The door clanged behind him as a new customer walked in.

"Get back to me as soon as you hear anything," Johnny said.

"Yeah," Nick said.

As Johnny turned from the counter, he sipped his coffee and spoke to the new patron.

"Make sure you get the coffee," he said. "It's fantastic."

# CHAPTER 4

DONUT AND FRESH coffee in hand, Johnny gave the day another shot. He stepped out onto the streets inhaling deeply through his nose like a bloodhound looking for a scent. He already knew where he was going, but there were several paths to take to get there. He needed to go the cemetery, keep his distance, and stake things out. Past experience told him that a proper stakeout often led to an easier go when staking hearts.

After inhaling one more time, Johnny took off, heading to the cemetery in almost the opposite way than he had the day before. This time he planned to head in from the north side, find a nice place to post up and watch.

Steam billowed from manhole covers and people bustled to and fro, often bumping into each other as they stared into the screens of their cellphones. Car horns honked and angry drivers swore out open windows. Music blasted from apartments above the storefronts and sidewalk cafes were alive with cigarette smoke. And above it all was the constant wail of sirens that annoyed most visitors to King City. Its permanent residents found it as comforting as a lullaby.

As he traversed the sidewalks toward the shadier side of town, the cracked concrete almost made him lose his balance. Johnny could picture the headline: 'Bounty Hunter Sprains Ankle on Unkempt City Streets.' He laughed at the thought, but his laughter was cut short when he heard a familiar scream.

Johnny checked his surroundings, yep, still heading in from the north side, and felt like pinching his own cheek. A familiar voice cried out.

"Get the fuck off me!"

Johnny rounded the corner and shook his head.

A gang of punks circled Snake Eyes, stomping and kicking him.

*So much for a lazy day of recon*, Johnny thought and took another sip of coffee, and took his time with the donut, savoring each bite. When it was gone, he crumpled the bag and tossed it in the can by the curb. It was a perfect toss, no rim at all.

"Ahem."

The punks looked around as one. Johnny peeled the lid off his to-go cup and watched the steam rise.

"Mind your business," said the one with purple hair.

The punk next to Purple Hair wore earrings up and down both ears. He was the biggest of the kids and his nose had been broken a few times. He took a step toward Johnny.

"Yeah," Earrings said. "Fuck off."

Johnny nodded and threw the hot coffee in Earrings' face. He followed it immediately with a fist and broke the guy's nose again. An elbow to the throat took out Purple Hair. Then Johnny's gun was out and pressed to another punk's forehead.

No one had seen him draw it.

"Who wants to die?" Johnny said.

The other two punks still standing ran. A dark, wet stain formed on the remaining guy's pants. Johnny pulled the barrel back an inch and gestured with it. The punk took the hint and split, running with knees wide around his damp crotch. Earrings and Purple Hair weren't getting up anytime soon.

"Thanks again," Snake Eyes said.

Johnny holstered his hand cannon.

"Damn it," Johnny said. "That was good coffee. What is it about you, Snake Eyes, that makes everyone want to kick your ass?"

Snake Eyes shrugged and tossed off a gap-toothed smile.

"Must be my charming personality."

Johnny glanced in the direction of the cemetery. He tapped his foot and thought for a minute.

"Snake Eyes," Johnny said, "how would you like to earn some money?"

"You're speaking my language."

After Johnny told the man what he had in mind,

Snake Eyes gathered up the few things he owned and followed Johnny to the cemetery.

"Vampires? No shit?"

"You had no idea?" Johnny asked.

"Uh-uh. I sleep in the shelter. You gotta get there before dark or they don't let you in."

"Lucky."

"Yeah," Snake Eyes said. "Might have to change my name to 'Sevens'."

They walked through the open cemetery gates. After a few hundred feet, birdsong and the muted rattle of leaves in the breeze replaced the sounds of the city. When they stopped, the two men stood before a large crypt. A brass plaque by the door said it belonged to the Cushing family.

The padlock was unlocked, though the steel loop hovered over the hole in the base, so if you weren't looking closely it appeared secure.

"You think they're in there?"

"That's what I hear," Johnny said.

Snake Eyes nodded. He put his back to the crypt and looked around. No one was in sight.

"Be careful in there," Snake Eyes said.

Johnny nodded, unhooking the lock and opening the door to the crypt. He went in.

The inside didn't stink like decay. Instead, it smelled stale. His first breath inside the tomb was the opposite of all those he'd taken that day. He left the door open a crack behind him. He didn't want to leave it wide open. Snake Eyes was probably a red flag enough; even Purple Hair or Earrings would know the dead were a tough crowd for a panhandler. He told Snake Eyes not to be obvious about being on the lookout, but considering Snake Eyes' record, Johnny thought the man might be getting his ass kicked in seconds.

Two steps into the crypt and Johnny changed his mind. He reached a hand out through the cracked door and grabbed Snake Eyes' arm.

"Ah Jesus! Fuck! Vampires!" Snake Eyes yelled.

"It's me," Johnny said.

"Oh, right. Well, what?"

"You're coming with me. I have a feeling if I don't keep you in my sight you'll wind up getting your ass kicked again."

Snake Eyes shrugged.

"You're right," he said, "I'm probably safer invading a vampire crypt with you than hanging out by myself."

Johnny paused for a moment, unable to tell if Snake Eyes was joking or not.

They shut the door behind them. Johnny pulled out a small flashlight and shone it around the crypt. The light illuminated little more than spider webs and dust. And a staircase heading down.

"After you," Snake Eyes said.

Johnny grinned and led the way. His light cut a small tunnel through the darkness and their feet crunched on leaves and pebbles and God knew what else as they descended the staircase. There was a peaked archway at the bottom. They stepped through that as well.

"Wait, stop," Snake Eyes whispered.

"What?"

"What if it's a trap?"

"What?"

"What if someone's been watching, just waiting to capture us?"

Johnny's blood ran cold. He hadn't considered this.

"People so unlucky aren't supposed to be that smart."

Snake Eyes didn't answer.

"All right then. If that's the case then we're already fucked, but still, let's make this quick."

They explored the dark crypt. Elevated coffins lined each side. Johnny tried to pry one open and couldn't. He noticed loose padlocks on all the coffins. The coffins must be locked from the inside but could also be locked from the outside. This meant they locked themselves in for protection, but someone, a leader or an overseer or someone had the capability to lock them in. Maybe to protect himself.

Weird.

Ten coffins lined each wall, twenty in total. Johnny didn't know how many of them actually housed a sleeping vampire, but prepared himself for battle with the maximum. Twenty, plus at least one other person; the one with the key to the outside locks. That was assuming this was the only crypt that housed vampires. If all of them did, Johnny could be looking at well over a hundred.

That would kind of suck.

One thing at a time.

Snake Eyes rapped on a coffin with his bare knuckles. It made a hollow gonging sound, but apparently wasn't enough to wake the dead.

"These coffins are funny," Snake Eyes said. "Ain't wood. Not sure what it is."

"It's wood, but it's a composite tempered with Kevlar. I've seen this before in Queen City. A grenade wouldn't even open these things."

"Damn."

Johnny and Snake Eyes crept through the crypt looking for any clue that would suggest who was in charge, who these vamps were, or what they wanted. Anything.

Johnny studied the coffins and the gaps in between. Snake Eyes wandered off on his own holding a Zippo with an open flame.

Johnny squatted and looked underneath some of the coffins. He ran his fingers over their surface looking for a button or a switch.

"Hey," Snake Eyes whispered. "I think I've found something."

Johnny jumped up and went to him.

"What?" Johnny asked.

"Can't you see the writing on the wall?" Snake Eyes asked.

"I'm not in the mood for riddles. Just tell me." Johnny grabbed Snake Eyes by the lapels.

"It's not a fucking riddle," Snake Eyes said. "Look at the fucking wall."

"Oh... Sorry," Johnny said, and shone his light on the wall.

There was indeed a message written in chalk on the crypt wall:

> *I hope you've rested well my friends. I've got a little surprise for you. For your dinner. I know you've grown tired of junkie punk blood. I've got something better for you. I'll see you at The Spot at midnight. And skip breakfast, I want you hungry.*

"So what do we do?" Snake Eyes asked.

"We find out where *The Spot* is, and then we go there."

Snake Eyes nodded. Johnny looked hard at him.

"But for now, we get out and hope no one locked us in. Because if they did, I'll kick your ass myself."

"Why? I just thought of it. I didn't do it."

Johnny squeezed the bridge of his nose. He nudged Snake Eyes forward.

"Just go. You can lead the way this time."

Snake Eyes grumbled under his breath but led them back the way they came. At the top of the stairs, he stopped and cursed.

"What?" Johnny asked.

"The door's closed. They locked us in, god damn

it. We're trapped like rats. We're gonna *die*."

Johnny pushed on the door and it swung open. Late morning sunshine and a light breeze filled the doorway.

"Oh. Well, it looked locked. Whatever."

Johnny clapped the other man on the shoulder just as the back of Snake Eyes' head exploded. Dropping into a crouch, Johnny drew his gun and fired as another bullet split the air above him. Forty feet away, Earrings fell back, blood spurting from his neck. He tried to stop the flow with his fingers, but it was futile.

"*Billy*!" Purple Hair yelled. His voice was tight with anguish. Purple Hair rounded on the crypt, firing wildly. Bits of marble flew off in all directions. When the boy's gun clicked on an empty chamber, Johnny stepped into the doorway and shot him in the forehead.

Three other Moron Brothers crashed through the bushes and charged. One had an enormous Bowie knife with a brass loop under the handguard. The kid spun it with a finger and the leather hilt smacked into his palm. Another punk gripped a black nightstick. It was the kind police used, based on the Okinawan tonfa. The third had brass knuckles.

Johnny registered these facts in under a second. Bowie Knife caught a bullet in the eye mid-spin and went down. Tonfa caught three in the chest and fell. Johnny holstered his gun and ducked the metal-covered fist. He came up hard with an uppercut to Brass Knuckles' nuts. The kid bent forward and Johnny met his face with a knee.

Drawing the gun again, Johnny stayed low and waited for the next attack. There wasn't one. He reloaded.

Johnny slid a ten dollar bill into Snake Eyes' shirt pocket.

"Sorry, man. That's on me."

With Brass Knuckles incapacitated, Johnny tossed him over his shoulder and carried him to a secluded parking structure near the cemetery. On the roof, Johnny used nylon cord to tie Brass Knuckles to a lamppost. Holding the two brass weapons, Johnny waited for the kid to come around. When he finally did, Johnny pitched one of them sidearm and hit the kid in his already broken nose.

"Ow. Shit, man. What the fuck?"

"Where's *The Spot*?"

"I don't know what you're talking about." the kid said. Blood trickled in his mouth, making him splutter.

Sighing, Johnny threw the other one, hitting the boy in the same place. The kid was crying now, great, big, wracking sobs.

"They'll kill me. If I tell you, they'll kill me."

"I'll kill you if you don't," Johnny said. "But, I'll take my time, you understand. Make it last a while. More fun that way."

Brass Knuckles hung limp on the post and cried

for a while. Johnny waited. Finally, the kid looked up, defeat in his eyes.

"Dodge Park," he said. "In the half-shell where they used to do concerts."

"Thank you," Johnny said. He started walking.

"Wait. You can't leave me here. They'll find me. They'll kill me. You gotta let me go."

"No. I don't."

Johnny left him there and went to the bakery.

"I left him a message, Johnny," Nick said. "I haven't heard back, I swear to Christ."

"Spilled my coffee, Nick. Think I could get another one?"

"Oh. Yeah. Sure, Johnny. You bet. You want another donut?"

"Life ain't that short, Nick."

Sitting at the counter, Johnny sipped the coffee. It was still too hot to drink, but he didn't care. When the door opened, Johnny glanced in the mirrored display case. When he saw who it was, he turned around and stood up.

Almost too fast to see, the man at the door flew at Johnny to tackle him. Johnny side-stepped and slammed the guy in the gut with a fist.

The man grinned, got up, and hugged Johnny.

"Damn, man. I'm gonna get you one of these days."

"Not likely," Johnny said, smiling back. "Thanks for coming, Gavin. Means a lot."

"Hey. When Nick said it was something Johnny

Headcase couldn't handle, I had to show up."

Nick shook his head, denying having said anything like that.

"I could handle it," Johnny said. "Probably. But, I thought you'd enjoy the chance to kill something you hadn't yet."

Gavin's eyes lit up.

"Ooh. Now, I'm even more intrigued. What is it? What are we hunting?"

"Vampires."

# CHAPTER 5

THE SUNSET SPLASHED orange and gold across the clouds. Gavin lay on his back, chewing a blade of grass. Beside him, Johnny triple-checked his pistol. A sheathed machete hung against his leg, strapped to his belt. With the grass clenched in his teeth, Gavin spoke.

"No wooden stakes?"

Johnny shook his head.

"No. Did some research. You'd be surprised what kind of stuff they have at the library. Seems the only way to kill a vampire is to separate the head from the body. Stakes just piss 'em off."

Gavin nodded.

"Good to know. But, why the gun, then?"

"I figure it'll slow 'em down a little. Nobody likes getting shot."

Gavin broke in.

"That's 'cause it hurts."

Johnny nodded.

"Plus, with aim like mine, I've been known to decapitate with one shot."

"Only you," Gavin snorted. "So, there are at least twenty of them?"

Johnny nodded.

"Maybe up to a hundred."

Gavin looked at him. He whistled.

Down the hill, a couple of Moron Brothers Johnny hadn't seen before dragged something onto the stage. Something under a sheet that wiggled and thrashed with hands and feet tied together.

Gavin stood up, sniffing the air.

"Johnny, I smell perfume."

"I don't," Johnny said.

"Yeah well, I hate to break it to you, Headcase, but some people are actually better at some things than you."

"But they're like half a mile away." Johnny watched the punks hoist the cloth.

Gavin inhaled deeply.

"Today, you've had one and a half cups of French roast coffee, had sex, have come into contact with the blood of at least four different people, and…" Gavin paused. "Maybe I'm crazy. Did you have a jelly donut?"

Johnny reddened.

"I only have one a year," he said to the grass.

"I smell something else under it all," Gavin said. "Headcase, you been wearing Cinnabar, too? I have to tell you, it's not really your scent."

Johnny's stomach churned. His mouth dried out.

*Cinnabar.*

"You all right?" Gavin asked. "I can about smell that donut coming back up."

Johnny glared at the stage. *How many times have you been shot?* His molars crushed together. *Is there anyone tougher than you?*

"Not so far," he mumbled.

"Whattya mean?"

Johnny looked at Gavin. "Forget it… Darla wears Cinnabar. She's my, I don't know, girlfriend, I guess. That's why you can smell it on me."

"Come on, man," Gavin said. "Might not be her. Lots of chicks wear Cinnabar."

Johnny didn't answer.

They sat in silence and watched the stage, Johnny with binoculars, Gavin with naked eyes.

"See that guy's nose?" Johnny said.

"That your handiwork?" Gavin asked.

"I gave him a thirty-dollar nose job."

"Do you just run around beating people up?" Gavin asked.

"Isn't that what you do?"

"Point taken," Gavin said. "Though, not usually people. Other stuff."

Johnny cocked an eyebrow at him.

"You know: monsters, that sort of thing."

"Monsters."

Gavin frowned.

"You make it sound dumb."

Johnny shrugged.

"Shut up, Headcase."

Thirty-Dollar Nose Job gave the other Moron Brothers a thumbs-up and bounded down the steps and into the dark park.

"So," Gavin said, "how are we going to play this?"

"We are going to kill all the vampires."

"Nice plan. Now?" Gavin asked.

"Unless you're scared."

"Dude, I killed a fucking dragon."

"No shit?"

"No shit. Six months ago, up in Alaska. What have you done lately? Broken some heroin junkie's nose."

"Asshole," Johnny laughed, but cut his laughter short as something happened down the hill.

A flock of vamps crowded the front of the stage. They moved fast. Faster than most people could follow. Of course, neither of the men watching were most people.

"What's going on?" Gavin asked.

"Shhhh. Just keep watching, don't look away, and don't move." Johnny only mouthed the words knowing Gavin's ears would be able to make sense of them.

Gavin tensed and stared straight at the stage.

Johnny's head jerked up and he glanced down at the blade of the machete he wore on his hip.

"Duck," he mouthed and Gavin hit the dirt.

Johnny wasted no time. He razored off a few millimeters of Gavin's hair as he drew his blade and swung in one motion.

"What the—" Gavin started.

Johnny caught the decapitated head before it hit the ground. The body crumpled to the grass.

Johnny glanced over his shoulder. The ceremony continued with no one looking back.

Gavin started to speak, ready to spring. Johnny silenced him. His hand went to the iron on his hip but pulled back. Instead, he cocked the severed head in his hand and threw it as hard as he could.

Ten feet away, it smacked another charging vamp square in the face, taking that one's head clean off. Both heads exploded like peeled oranges smashed together.

Johnny had one hell of an arm.

"Okay, it's safe. I got 'em," Johnny said and hunkered in the grass.

"Okay, what the hell was that?" Gavin asked.

"You needed a haircut."

Gavin ran a hand through his hair and shook his head.

"I took out two vamps." Johnny shrugged. "And I did it without alerting the rest."

"Yeah, I mean, I get it, but how? I didn't hear *or* smell them. That's weird for me."

"I've got a couple of super senses myself, just in a different way."

"What else you got?"

"You'll see," Johnny said and the two of them looked back to the ritual.

The vampires on stage unwrapped the shrouded form with the enthusiasm of children at Christmas. Johnny and Gavin crept toward the stage in silence. At center stage, the vampires peeled back the final layer of sheet revealing the prize inside. A woman. She thrashed against the ropes that held her wrists and yelled into her gag, making angry muffled noises.

Now that they were close, Johnny could smell Cinnabar, too.

*Darla.*

Doing a quick head count, Johnny estimated around fifteen vampires, plus the two Moron Brothers. Gavin put his hand on Johnny's arm, holding up a palm and putting a finger to his lips. Johnny waited, keeping an eye on the stage as the vampires moved closer to Darla.

Without a sound, Gavin slid off his T-shirt and pulled down his sweats and underwear. He stepped out of his slip-on shoes and stood naked in the park.

Johnny waggled his eyebrows and pursed his lips for a kiss. Gavin grinned and shook his head. Lunging forward, Gavin's body rippled. In under a second, he was a pony-sized, brown wolf.

Leaping thirty feet onto the stage, Gavin twisted his head to one side as he passed a vampire. Using his teeth, the wolf tore off the undead head. The body stood upright for a moment, swaying as the head rolled across the stage floor.

Fourteen vampires and three humans turned as one and looked at the wolf. Wolf Gavin growled low and menacing. He got Johnny's attention and made a show of closing his eyes before the fight. He sniffed, then snorted. Gavin could still smell them. His ears flicked back and forth, tracking movement.

As the attackers closed on him, Gavin feinted right and attacked left, locking his jaws on what felt like an arm. He worried it like a dog, back and forth, shredding the undead meat. Up that close, the scent made him sneeze.

From Gavin's left, strong hands gripped him. One held his ear and the other the loose skin on the back of his neck. The icy fingers tightened, locked like a vise. Pushing his front paws into the stage, Gavin tried to shove up and back to dislodge the vampire.

But before he could, two hot spikes, an inch or so apart, plunged into the wolf's neck. The bite punctured an artery and Gavin's blood flowed through the fangs into the vampire. From all around, vampires piled on the werewolf, holding him down and feeding on him.

Gavin bit clean through the bone of the arm he held in his jaws. That vampire shrieked and clutched his stump, face twisted by pain and rage. Then, his expression turned to surprise as his head fell backward, separated from his body by the blade of a machete.

Johnny Headcase waded into the bloody cloud of vampires, guided by instinct honed by years of combat. The undead fell to his blade one at a time as Johnny fought his way to the wounded wolf. The Moron Brothers leaped in to join the fray, but with his left hand, Johnny drew his piece and shot each man in the face. Flipping the pistol by the trigger guard, Johnny slid it back into its holster.

All fifteen vampire bodies were now separated from their heads, dead for the second time. Gavin's body, human now, lay unbreathing on the concrete floor of the stage in a pool of blood.

"Hopefully your favorite song was *Bullet in the Head*," Johnny said as he wiped the machete blade clean on a Moron Brother's *Rage Against the Machine* t-shirt and sheathed it. He stepped over the corpses and pulled the gag down from Darla's mouth.

"Hey baby," Johnny said. "Sorry I was almost too late."

"Oh no, Johnny," Darla said. "You *are* too late."

She flexed the muscles in her arms and legs, bursting through her bonds. Grabbing Johnny by the collar with both hands, Darla bared her fangs and lunged in for the kill.

Johnny's gun was out, but he couldn't get the angle to make the shot.

"Damn it," he grunted, leaning back from his ex-living girlfriend. She was nearly as strong as he was now.

Johnny shoved her back with every bit of strength and gained a few inches of space.

"Darla?"

"What?"

"We had a good thing, but I can't deal with who you are now—what you are. I'm gonna have to pass on that rain check."

She snarled and lunged, knocking his hands away.

Her fangs were at his neck, the tips poking hard against the skin, when she was slammed to one side, hard. A wolf pounced on her, pinning her down. She thrashed under him, jaw snapping, looking for something to bite. Gavin dipped his snout down and clamped his jaws on her throat. He ripped her head off at the root.

Gavin stood, morphing to human as he did. He looked at Johnny, wiping the blood from his mouth.

"Can we get some food, man? I'm famished."

Johnny looked around at all the dead bodies still leaking blood. Hell, in a few minutes it would be ankle deep. He stared for a lingering second. First at Darla's body, then her decapitated head.

"You all right?" Gavin asked putting a hand on Johnny's shoulder.

"Yeah," Johnny said. "I think she was cheating on me anyway."

"Wow, man. Talk about insult to injury."
Johnny clapped him on the shoulder.
"All right, let's eat. I know just the place."

Now, man, I'll about *bust* in fury."

Johnny *tapped* him on the shoulder.

"Al man, tell you, I know, just the place."

# CHAPTER 6

JOHNNY SAT across from Gavin at the buffet, studying his friend. Gavin was elbow deep in his seventh plate piled high with steak and ribs and a whole chicken. Soup bowls filled with ketchup, barbecue sauce and Heinz 57 surrounded him. Gavin did not use silverware. He just picked up big hunks of meat and devoured them, occasionally spitting out bones or gristle. He itched absently at the back of his neck between bites.

"You know, you probably could've saved us a lot of time if you'd just eaten my girlfriend and those vampires," Johnny said.

"Gross, man. They would have tasted terrible."

"What about the punks?"

"Yeah, no. I'm a werewolf not a cannibal, Headcase."

Gavin chewed and kept itching.

"Well, hurry the hell up. I'm bored and people are staring. You're gonna get us kicked out."

"Johnny Headcase, fearless bounty hunter, scared of getting kicked out of Big Bob's All You Can Eat

Meat Buffet." Gavin went into a sarcastic commercial voice. "You can't beat our meat. Come to Big Bob's," he said, flecks of meat flying from his lips.

"Hey, I come here a lot," Johnny said.

Gavin grinned around a mouthful of ribs.

"Of course you do. It's all you can eat."

"Just finish and quit scratching your neck, you're freaking me out."

"Hang on. I'm working on something. Almost," Gavin said digging his nails in, "*got* 'em." He put his bloody hand on the table. In his palm sat two large vampire fangs. He went to throw them on a spare plate as a waitress came to clear them away.

"No," Johnny said, "Save those, you never know."

"We're uh…" the waitress started, visibly nervous. "We're about to be closing up for the night, so could you maybe finish up?" Her voice carried a hint of honey that made Gavin's ears perk up. He glanced at her name tag, which read Isabella.

"Yes," Johnny said, "we were just leaving after this plate, weren't we, Gavin?"

"I haven't even had dessert," Gavin muttered.

"Do you, uh, want me to take those teeth?"

Johnny picked them up, wiped them on a napkin, and put them in his shirt pocket. Isabella looked mildly disgusted.

"I'll hang onto them," Johnny said.

"Right." She dropped the check and left.

"Waitresses at the buffet. What's the world coming to?" Gavin asked.

"Shut up," Johnny said. "You got any money?"

"Nope," Gavin said. He shrugged. "No pockets."

"Christ."

"Hey, you called me to help you, remember?"

Johnny chuckled and pulled out his two rolls of quarters and left them on top of the check.

"Man, I hate spending these," he said. "You still want dessert?"

"Yes. I do, badly, but we're broke."

"It's cool," Johnny said. "I know a place, and I know a guy."

"Nick's is closed. It's, like, after midnight."

"We're going to a diner. They've got the best apple pie you've ever tasted, and it's going to be served with a side of information."

"Sounds like this is going to turn into another fight," Gavin said.

"Yeah, it might. Maybe even a kidnapping. Just promise you won't order the coffee. It tastes like liquid shit."

# CHAPTER 7

JOHNNY PUSHED open the glass door of the diner with his foot, holding it for Gavin with his heel. When both were inside, Thirty-Dollar Nose Job put up both hands, palms out, and backed as far away as he could. Plates rattled on the rack behind him as he touched his injured nose with the tip of one finger. When Nose Job spoke, his voice was filtered through a pronounced nasal twang.

"I told you everything I knew. I swear I did."

Johnny nodded.

"Relax, kid. Just here for the pie."

"We're out of apple," the kid said.

Johnny slammed a fist down so hard the cash register *ching*ed and opened. His voice was calm, icy.

"No apple. Unbelievable."

Walking around the counter, Gavin passed the kid. When he did, Gavin shot him a smile with red-stained teeth with tiny bits of meat stuck in the gaps. Pouring himself a cup of coffee, Gavin leaned on the counter a few feet from Nose Job.

Johnny cut two pieces of strawberry rhubarb pie.

"Fucking rhubarb," Johnny muttered.

"On... on the house."

Eyebrows raised, Johnny grinned at the kid and handed a piece to Gavin.

"Thank you kindly," Johnny said.

The two toughest men in King City ate pie in silence. Sweat formed on Nose Job's blue hairline, and dripped down the side of his face. He blinked. When his eyes opened they were looking down the barrel of a gun.

"Jesus Christ, Johnny," Gavin said.

"What?"

"This really is bad coffee."

Without taking his eyes off the kid, Johnny gave a slight nod and smirked.

"Here's how we're going to do this," he said. "You'll tell me who pulls the strings in this vampire operation and who got Darla involved. I'm all out of patience, puke face, so you have thirty seconds. Then, I pull the trigger. Twenty-nine."

Nose Job's eyes went wide. He told them everything. It took longer than thirty seconds, but Johnny let that slide. When Nose Job finished, Johnny eased the pistol into its holster. The kid slid down the wall and sat on the floor. Tears fell down his cheeks, but he made no sound.

"Thanks for the pie," Gavin said. He dumped the coffee in the sink and set the dirty cup in a bus tub. Snatching a toothpick from the dispenser, Gavin followed Johnny outside. Gavin picked at steak bits and strawberry seeds and waited for Johnny to say something. The other man's brow furrowed over an angry frown. When both ends of the toothpick were soggy and frayed, Gavin flicked it over the curb. He waited some more. Finally, Johnny looked at him.

"It galls me, man."

Gavin kept his mouth shut.

"I mean," Johnny went on, "Darla was no sucker for a pretty face."

"That's kind of obvious."

"Cheap shot, Gavin."

The werewolf shrugged. Staring ahead, Johnny went on.

"What I mean is, she was more interested in who you were than what you look like, you know? Darla wasn't superficial at all. So, this asshole vampire Nose Job was talking about must have had some kind of hold over her."

"'Nose Job'?"

"In my head, I name all these clowns based on their salient features."

"You know, for a tough guy, you sound kind of like a dictionary."

"I read some," Johnny said with a shrug.

The streetlights illuminated the blood and filth on the two men. Gavin reached out and flicked a piece of someone off Johnny's coat.

"I need a shower. You?" Gavin asked.

"Nah. Seeing you naked once was plenty for me."

Gavin laughed.

"Okay. I guess we could take turns."

They ambled toward Johnny's place. The few people out at that hour gave them a wide berth.

"I think Isabella likes me," Gavin said, out of the blue.

"Who?"

"The waitress at the buffet. She was giving me the eye. I'm gonna ask her out."

"If we survive tonight's party with the master vampire."

Gavin cocked his head to the side.

"How does one get to be a 'master' vampire?"

Johnny shrugged.

"Don't know. Maybe you have to put in ten thousand hours as a vampire?"

"Ha! Seriously, though."

"Master vampire is the vampire that made all the other vampires."

"You learn that at the library, too?"

"Yup."

# CHAPTER 8

JOHNNY YAWNED as he pulled open the door to the lobby of his apartment complex.

"You getting old on me, Headcase?" Gavin asked.

"We've killed like a hundred people today, not to mention I lost a good friend and a girlfriend."

"It was more like twenty people, Headcase. And, I wouldn't even call most of them 'people'." Gavin jabbed a finger into Johnny's ribs. "Also, and this is the real killer, you had a jelly donut."

"Yeah, well, not all of us can eat eight plates of meat and keep a cut figure."

"Johnny Headcase admits defeat again. I don't even know you anymore." Gavin slapped him high on the back. "Aren't you going to get your mail?" He asked as the two of them climbed the stairs to Johnny's third floor apartment.

"Fuck the mail," Johnny said.

They sidestepped discarded trash and beer cans

in the rundown tenement. The sounds of fornication emanated from the complex's paper-thin walls.

"Jesus, Headcase, it reeks in here."

"See, I guess your super senses have flaws too. It just smells like home to me. I'd like to get a new place, but bounty hunting ain't what it used to be…"

Johnny halted and put a hand on Gavin's chest, stopping him.

The door to Johnny's apartment was hanging by one hinge.

"This day just won't quit," Gavin whispered, and cracked his knuckles.

Johnny nodded and unsheathed his machete, not wanting to wake his whole building with gunfire in the middle of the night.

"Stay here," Johnny whispered.

Gavin looked hurt and puzzled.

"I've seen you fight. No way you can do it without breaking all my shit."

"That's probably true," Gavin conceded. He pulled out his cellphone.

"No money, no pockets, where did you even get that phone from?"

Gavin grinned.

"Nevermind, I don't want to know."

"All right, I'll just sit out here and play Candy Crush. Give me the all clear when it's, you know, all clear."

Johnny rolled his eyes, raised the machete and crept through the doorway.

Dirty moonlight and dirtier streetlight filtered through his broken blinds, casting wicked shadows across the room. Nothing moved. Nothing made a sound. Johnny squinted and looked around the living room. He didn't see anything but he felt it.

Then he heard it. A small, faint, sound came from his bedroom. He took a deep breath and crept across the carpet and stood in his bedroom doorway, calculating.

Johnny's breath caught when he saw disarray, Darla's blood, and broken things in his bedroom. Splintered wood and shattered glass littered the carpet. It reeked of Cinnabar. A bottle of the perfume lay broken in the corner of the bedroom.

A dim glow appeared from under his bed along with an audible vibration.

"Fuck," a voice muttered.

"Yep. Bad time for a text message. You might as well come out. Do it slow or I'll cut your head off," Johnny said and flipped on the light. "Gav, you can come in, all my shit's broken already anyway."

"Hang on, I got three more moves."

"Goddamn it," Johnny muttered. Then, "You, out. Now."

First he saw hands, nails painted pink, rings on every finger. Then wrists with several bracelets clicking together.

"I'm coming. Don't shoot or stab me or

whatever," she said slithering out from under the bed.

She stood up, dressed in a black skirt and black tank top, black bra straps, black eyeliner, black lipstick, black mascara, black socks, black ass-stomper boots. Pink hair. Pink belt.

"I like the way the belt ties the outfit together," Johnny said.

She ignored him and rubbed her hands against her shirt. Dust puffed in the air.

"Jesus," she said. "Ever heard of a vacuum cleaner? They're like forty bucks at K-Mart."

"You don't get to break into my apartment and complain," Johnny said.

"Fine," she said. "But seriously, dude." She plucked a pube-ridden hunk of dryer lint from her left boob and dropped it to the floor. Johnny watched it fall.

"You could've put that in the trashcan," Johnny said, pointing to it with the machete.

"Easy, Headcase. The door was already kicked off the hinges, and you don't have to believe me, but I had nothing to do with this." She gestured to the blood and the broken things.

"How do you know my name? Who are you? And what the fuck are you doing here?"

"My name is Siren. I'm a succubus, and I'm here to fuck you and suck out your soul." She purred and batted thick black eyelashes.

"I don't believe you."

She sighed.

"No shit, Sherlock. Man, detective skills like that, I can't believe you haven't killed McBride yet. You're famous, Headcase. Everyone knows your damn name."

He pinched his nose and squeezed his eyes shut. He was lost. Also, the mystery girl wasn't exactly hideous.

"Gavin, get in here," he yelled to the hallway.

"Hang on, bro, I just caved and bought a few more moves."

Johnny shook his head. "Christ."

The girl giggled.

Something thumped behind the closed bathroom door. Johnny's gun was in his hand.

"What the hell?"

The girl put a pink finger to her black lips.

"Vampire. I thought I killed him," she whispered.

"Did you cut his head off?"

She shook her head.

"Then you probably didn't kill him. Now who's the amateur?" Johnny took off for the bathroom. "Don't even think about leaving," he said. "My buddy outside is a werewolf."

"A werewolf who's addicted to Candy Crush. Scary."

Johnny shrugged.

"He killed a dragon."

"No shit?"

Johnny stared at the door between the bedroom

and the bathroom for a few seconds and then said, "Pay attention, Pinkie. This is how we do it in the pros."

Switching the gun to his left hand, he drew his machete. He closed his eyes for show and sliced the blade through the air, through the door, and through the vampire's neck. They heard a splash and a puddle of red spread under the door.

"Bet you twenty bucks his head landed in the toilet."

"You can't even afford a vacuum cleaner," she shot back.

"Open the top dresser drawer," Johnny said.

She did and her eyes narrowed.

"It's just full of rolls of quarters," she said. "Hundreds of them."

"Yeah well, sometimes money helps people talk. Tell you what, if the head isn't in the toilet, I'll let you go, no questions asked."

"And give me twenty bucks."

"Fine. But if it's in, you owe me some answers."

"Deal." She nodded and opened the door.

The bathroom door resisted against the headless body obstructing the path, but the girl shouldered it open.

She almost slipped in the blood as she kicked the body to the side and stared into the toilet. The head was wedged between the toilet bowl and the lid.

The pink-haired girl looked at Johnny with a smirk.

Gavin stormed into the apartment.

"Dude, I finally beat level 243. Fuckin' *A*." He stomped a foot hard on the floor and slapped Johnny on the back, then registered the headless body. "What'd I miss?"

The vibration from Gavin's stomp shook the apartment just enough to unstick the severed head and roll it into the toilet bowl.

*Kerplunk.*

"You've gotta be fuckin' kidding me," the girl said.

Johnny looked at the girl with a smirk of his own.

Gavin looked at her. His eyebrows climbed up as his eyes slid down, taking her in head to toe.

"Who's this?"

"A succubus. She was just about to tell me her name, weren't you?"

She puffed out her reddening cheeks and muttered, "Lydia. My name is Lydia."

"Nice to meet you Lydia," Johnny offered his hand. She didn't shake it. "I know you already know me, but this is my friend Gavin."

"'Sup," Gavin said. She ignored his offered hand too. He looked at her pink hair. "Does the carpet match the drapes?"

"Nobody likes a sore loser," Johnny said.

"I'll answer three questions," Lydia said, "then I'm out of here."

"I'll let you know when the conversation is over," Johnny said.

"Three questions, then I bet I'll be gone before you even know it. And that, Johnny Headcase, is a bet I won't lose."

"We'll see about that," Gavin said.

"Okay, fine, whatever, but can we not do this in the bathroom? That blood smell is about to make me gag."

Johnny didn't have much furniture so the three of them just stood in a weird triangle in the middle of his bedroom while they talked.

"Okay," Johnny said. "Who are you?"

She shrugged.

"I'm like you, a bounty hunter who wants to clear King City of the vampires."

"What are you doing here, in my apartment?" Johnny asked.

"I'm here looking for clues, dude. I was at The Spot earlier and I saw you, but you didn't see me. I saw what they did to your girlfriend. That was ugly."

"Yeah," Johnny said.

"Then I saw what you did to his girlfriend," Lydia said to Gavin.

"Yeah, that was ugly too," Gavin said. "Had to be done, though." He held up vampire fangs. "Plus, I got souvenirs. Are you really a succubus?"

"You wish."

"That doesn't count against my three," Johnny said.

"Fair enough," Lydia said. "Anyway, when I found out who she was and her ties to you, I thought maybe I could catch a lead at your apartment. When I got here the door was already destroyed along with half of your shit. I was looking for a diary, a cellphone, anything to give me a tip. Believe it or not, Headcase, we're chasing the same monster, but I'll be damned if I'm splitting my bounty."

Johnny opened his mouth to answer and ask something else.

"Careful cowboy, you've only got one more question."

"You're bluffing."

"I assure you I'm not," Lydia said.

Gavin and Johnny whispered to each other, strategizing the final question.

"Three questions aren't very many," Gavin said.

"True, but perhaps we'll meet again."

"Okay," Johnny said. "Who is McBride?"

"The person I'm hunting. The person you're hunting, I assume. I say person because I don't know if they are male or female. What I do know is he or she is responsible for creating the vampire epidemic in King City. I don't know for sure, but I think it's to create super-powered third shift workers. They do twice the work with extra strength and fly under the radar because no one in an authority position gives a shit about people that thrive at night. McBride can run a construction crew that builds shit twice as fast as a regular crew. You've seen the new soccer stadium?"

Johnny nodded.

"Yeah," Lydia said, "they built it in a week. It should've taken months. But people are dying, disappearing, because the vampires have to be fed, which is where the two of us come in. But to tell you the truth, I care a lot more about the one hundred dollars a head I'm getting for vampires than I do the people of King City, which is why I'm out of here. I'll see you around, gentlemen, and Johnny." She winked.

"Wait. A hundred dollars a head? I'm only getting sixty. Who are you working for?" Johnny asked.

"Uh-uh. You're out of questions, big fella. Tell you what," Lydia said, "if I crack anything cool off this, I'll be in touch." She pulled what appeared to be Darla's cell phone from her pocket. "I guess that's only fair."

"Give me that," Johnny reached for the phone.

Lydia took a deep breath and closed her eyes. She pushed a button on the phone and a spray shot out, straight into the faces of Gavin and Johnny.

They screamed and clawed at their faces. Lydia walked out of the room and said, "Decoy phone. Pepper spray. Guys always fall for that one. Don't feel bad. But I'll keep my word."

Their eyes burned. Their noses were scorched. Their throats hurt.

"Goddamn it," Johnny yelled.

"Fuckin' *ow*," Gavin yelled.

They heard Lydia giggling as she walked out of the apartment.

# CHAPTER 9

JOHNNY STAGGERED into the kitchen and rinsed his eyes with water until the burning stopped.

"Your turn," he said, turning to Gavin. The werewolf shrugged.

"I'm good."

Johnny gave Gavin a long look through sore, teary eyes. There didn't appear to be anything wrong at all.

"You're a dick. You know that, right?"

Gavin shrugged.

"Not my fault I'm a werewolf."

"I'm betting you were a dick before you were a werewolf."

"Maybe," Gavin said, "but I'm a much bigger dick now. Speaking of, dibs on the shower."

"You want to help me clean up the dead vampire first?"

Gavin sighed.

"I guess. Not much point of showering and *then*

doing it."

The two men rolled the body in Johnny's blanket, then unrolled it again when they remembered the head. Gavin fished it out of the toilet and tossed it face-down on the body's crotch.

"Look. He's blowing himself."

Johnny shook his head.

"What, are you twelve?"

"Mentally, yeah. Right around there."

Opening the window, Johnny looked into the alley. A cat scavenged for scraps near the open dumpster, but it was otherwise deserted.

"Lucky," he mumbled, as he lifted the dead vampire and tossed it out. It fell, still wrapped up, and landed right in the dumpster, scaring at least one life out of the cat. Johnny brushed off his hands, wondering if the trash pick-up guys would notice. Behind him, he could hear the shower running.

When both men were clean and dressed—Gavin in one of Johnny's plain white T-shirts and a pair of chinos from a thinner time in Johnny's life—they looked around at what was left of the apartment. With a sigh, Johnny pulled an empty gym bag from the closet and dumped all the rolls of quarters in it. When Johnny kicked the wall vent, the panel fell off. Reaching in up to his elbow, Johnny pulled out another gym bag and tossed it to Gavin.

"What's this?"

"Hardware," Johnny said.

Gavin opened the bag and whistled.

"It's like the whole damn hardware store," he said. "You planning on fighting an army?"

"Yeah. Aren't you?"

"Hell yeah."

"I was tired of this place anyway," Johnny said, shouldering the forty pounds of change. They left.

Stepping outside in the crisp night air, both men paused to take a breath. Gavin cough-snorted in the middle of his and then sniffed rapidly, turning his head side to side.

"What is it, boy?" Johnny asked. "Did Timmy fall in the well?"

Gavin stopped sniffing and glared at the other man.

"And you call me a dick?"

"Yeah, well. Seriously, what do you smell?"

"That," Gavin said, pointing across the street.

Vampires. Forty or fifty at least, climbing from the shadows of the alleys and buildings nearby.

"Damn it. I just got clean," Johnny said. Setting down the bag of quarters with a heavy *thunk*, he drew his pistol with one hand and the machete with the other. Next to him, Gavin growled low and menacing. Like the tide coming in, the vampires poured across the street.

Ten feet from the two men, they stopped.

Johnny glanced at Gavin, who shrugged. The vampires looked frozen where they stood.

"Maybe it's your breath," Johnny said.

"Nuh-uh. I used your toothbrush."

"Aw, man. You didn't. Really?"

"No. I'm messing with you. I put toothpaste on my finger and used that."

"Classy."

They waited for something to happen. After a moment, something did. From down the street, the distinct click of boot heels got louder.

"When were you going to tell me we had company?" Johnny asked.

"I didn't hear anything before you, which is nuts, because my hearing is *way* better than yours."

The clicking got nearer and a figure flowed from the night. It was a man who appeared to be in his late forties. He wore tailored grey pants and collar shirt under a sweater vest. The noisy boots were glossy black leather that gleamed in the streetlight. Passing the ranks of undead, the man stroked one's jaw in a proprietary way. When he reached Johnny and Gavin, the man turned to them with a dazzling, movie star smile.

"Gentlemen," he said. "So nice to finally meet you both."

"Mr. McBride, I presume," Gavin said.

The master vampire tossed off a dramatic bow, swinging one manicured hand wide.

"At your service. I see my reputation precedes me. As does yours, of course."

Johnny blew air out of his nostrils in a quick, amused snort.

"Why aren't they killing us?" he asked.

"I don't want them to," McBride said. "You see, despite the, ah, *difficulties* you and your werewolf friend have been causing me lately, I genuinely like you."

"For a meal, you mean," Gavin said.

"Oh no. I prefer to dine on prey animals. There are so very many of them in King City. But you two are predators, like me. You'd taste awful."

"Uh huh," Johnny said. "Okay. I'll buy that for the moment, but I still don't get what you're doing here with this army of stiffs."

Gavin laughed out loud at *stiffs*.

"I have come to parlay," McBride said. "To offer you a deal."

"Not interested," Gavin said.

"Hang on." Johnny put his hand on Gavin's chest.

McBride flashed his pearly whites. Two of them were a bit long and pointy, but the rest looked perfect.

"Headcase, you don't want to deal with this guy," Gavin said. "He's an asshole. Just look at him. He's got a manicure for God's sake."

"Sure he is, but it's still several hours before dawn and we're a bit outnumbered. I mean, we could maybe take 'em, but our odds aren't great."

Gavin's lips moved as he counted the vampires. Forty-seven, plus McBride. With a somewhat petulant frown, he shrugged.

"Fine. Whatever. We'll listen. But, if we don't like your deal, we kill you first."

"Perfectly reasonable," McBride said. "My proposal is quite simple: we share King City. You don't try to kill me or get in the way of my construction projects and I give you each two percent of profit."

"How many dollars is that likely to translate into?" Johnny asked.

"Nine or ten million annually," said McBride. "Each."

Gavin whistled. Johnny looked at the werewolf and raised an eyebrow. Gavin twisted his lip and shrugged again.

"What's in it for you?" Gavin asked.

McBride shrugged.

"It's a matter of expediency, gentlemen. It costs me far less to buy your cooperation than to continually have to repair the damage you seem intent on inflicting on my property. This way, we can all get rich, and nobody else gets hurt."

"We'd like to think about it," Johnny said.

"Of course. I'll expect your answer in seventy-two hours. It's been a pleasure."

McBride reached out to shake hands. Neither mortal moved to accept, and McBride shrugged it off with his Hollywood smile. He slowly strode away, disappearing into the night. Johnny and Gavin looked at the forty-seven unmoving vampires.

"Time to go?" Gavin asked.

Johnny nodded and picked up the bag of rolled quarters. They backed away, keeping an eye on the frozen stiffs. They had only gotten about twenty feet when the vampires started moving again. The undead heads all turned, necks creaking toward the two men.

# CHAPTER 10

"Aw, DAMN IT," Johnny said, drawing his machete. "I guess when the master leaves, the rest get to do what they want."

Gavin grinned. "And, what they want is to fight." He undressed. When he finished, someone whistled. Forty-nine heads turned toward the sound.

"It's not a party until someone gets naked," Lydia said. She had two long, curving blades in her hands.

Gavin wolfed out and shook his fur.

"Yeah," Johnny said. "I like these odds better."

Before Johnny finished his sentence, Lydia dashed and joined up with the two men.

"That was pretty fast," Johnny said.

"Just wait," she grinned.

Gavin roared.

The vampires advanced, hissing and flashing sharp fangs, red eyes radiating in the dark street.

Johnny grabbed Lydia by the shoulders and spoke to her like she was a child.

"Now remember," he said, "you've got to cut their heads off. Otherwise you're going to get us all killed."

Even Johnny could make out Gavin's 'easy Headcase' face in wolf form as he turned to the impending onslaught.

"Just try to keep up, grandpa," Lydia said.

"Take it easy. I'm only…" but she was already gone.

Then both their jaws dropped open.

A flash of pink, black, and blood-red cut through the herd like a weed whacker. The heads of vampires leapt from their shoulders as Lydia sprang from target to target like a game of connect the dots.

"Damn," Johnny said to himself. Then to Gavin, "Maybe you should just put your clothes back on." When there was no answer, Johnny turned and saw he was only speaking to Gavin's discarded clothes. He looked back to the crowd of vampires, now mowed down in half, heads still hanging in the air, necks spewing blood like erupting volcanos.

Gavin moved slightly slower but still fast as hell in a furry blur, liberating the heads of those that remained. The two cut twin paths straight through the center of the group.

Johnny looked at his machete and his legs. He was strong and smart, but couldn't compete with that kind of speed. Christ, at this rate, the pair would have all the vampires killed before he got in the mix.

He raised his gun, wondering if those two could travel faster than a speeding bullet. Then he realized the dorkiness of what he'd just thought, and wanted to punch himself.

The vampires on the outskirts of the group fanned out to avoid Lydia's cutting and Gavin's ripping.

Just to make a point, Johnny squeezed off two quick shots. The surviving vampires flanked him, then circled him, and he wished he had the duo with him inside the closing circle. He trusted a phalanx more than he trusted himself.

The vampires tightened their perimeter. Johnny counted fifteen of them, unscathed by the attacks of Gavin and Lydia, and they looked pissed off.

"You need some help, old man?" Lydia jeered, and slapped Gavin's paw high five. "That's how we do it in the pros."

"Bitch," Johnny muttered under his breath.

Gavin's roar sounded just like laughter.

"You could help," Johnny yelled as they came in closer.

"We did." Lydia yelled. "We each took out our portion." She smiled. Blood coated her body.

Gavin changed back into human form, shivering and covering his junk.

Lydia laughed and Johnny fought a grin. Then she dashed. She sprinted gracefully through the closing circle and grabbed Gavin's clothes.

"All right, assholes," Johnny said. "I'm glad you think this is funny."

Lydia giggled. "If I would've known it'd take him this long I would've brought a six pack."

Red-faced, Johnny dipped down and pulled a special gun from the duffel bag containing his arsenal. It was long with a wide, flat barrel. It looked like it shot pancakes. What it actually shot was spinning buzz saws. Under the barrel, a serrated double-bladed bayonet protruded like a battle-axe.

Just before the first vampire tried to bite him, Johnny blocked the blow with the barrel of the gun and pulled the trigger. A high whizzing sound cut the air as the blade cut through the vampire's head. Before its head hit the ground, Johnny racked another blade in the chamber, stomped over the falling body and jammed the bayonet through the neck of a nearby vampire.

Two down.

Thirteen to go.

One grabbed him from behind and tried to sink his teeth into Johnny's neck. Johnny flung his heel up and caught the vamp square in the balls. The vamp fell to his knees and Johnny ripped his head off. He spiked it like a football and screamed a belligerent war cry.

A hundred yards or so away, Lydia and Gavin gave him their best golf clap.

"Who else wants some?" Johnny screamed and

shot another vampire through the neck with a buzz saw. The blade carried the severed head like a cannibal's dinner on a plate until they both struck a brick wall.

Several more vampires closed on him.

"Watch this," Johnny yelled to Gavin and Lydia.

Johnny crouched, held the bayonet out and spun on his back like a break dancer. The blade cut through the legs of all the vampires within its range. Their torsos all fell between their own severed knees.

Everyone one knew Johnny had a hell of an arm, but no one knew that his feet packed a wallop too. In another life, he could've been a soccer star or buried seventy-yard field goals in the NFL. But today, he settled for kicking heads off bodies.

While the vampires hissed in pain at their severed limbs, Johnny kicked each one in the face. Some of them took two or three kicks, but in a few more minutes he'd decapitated them all and stomped their remains into Jell-O.

Panting, he looked to Gavin with a giant grin on his face. Gavin was looking down at his phone. So was Lydia. Johnny was pissed.

"Hey," Johnny yelled. "Show's over here. What the fuck?"

Gavin yawned.

"I'm almost through level 244," he said.

"I've actually got you on a stopwatch Headcase, and it ain't pretty."

"Goddamn it," he yelled.

"Your six," Lydia said.

Johnny turned and kicked another vamp straight in the balls. Johnny put everything he had into that kick. All his shit being broken, losing his girlfriend, and most of all Gavin and Lydia's indifference. Johnny nailed him so hard and with such force he felt the poor fucker's balls pop. Johnny's leg lifted through the vampire's pelvic bone. Johnny's foot just kept going and all of a sudden it was through the top of the guy's head, splitting the vampire into a pair of gooey, bloody halves.

"Whoa," Gavin said, looking up from his phone.

"Fatality," Lydia said.

"Fuck. I think I pulled my groin," Johnny said, and fell to the pavement clutching his leg.

The last two vampires bore down on him.

"Dude, you've done nothing but pull that thing since you were in seventh grade," Gavin said.

"I'm fucking serious, Gavin," Johnny said.

He grabbed for the buzz saw gun but it was outside his reach. His leg lay useless, a dead weight. He had no weapons anywhere near him and the vamps were about to tear into his neck and torso. He threw a punch that had little behind it as he struggled on the ground.

"Seriously?" Lydia asked.

Johnny glanced at her. Saw her slide one of her bracelets off and slap it against her thigh. The thing grew to the size of a Frisbee, but it didn't look like a

Frisbee. It looked like one of his saw blades. With a snap of her wrist, Lydia let the blade loose. Just as the vamps were about to take their first bite, Lydia's chakram cut both their heads off.

# CHAPTER 11

"C'MON HEADCASE, you're embarrassing yourself," she said, jogging over and helping him to his feet.

Johnny took her hand and Gavin joined them, staring at his phone screen. He tripped on a body, recovered, tapped the phone a couple more times, grinned and put it in his pocket.

Lydia made a dramatic show of tapping the stop button on the stopwatch app on her cell phone.

Johnny and Gavin both cowered and shielded their eyes as she did so.

"Relax guys," she said, "I'm just calculating how long it took Johnny to take out those vamps, and working out a formula to subtract my help."

Gavin laughed.

Johnny didn't.

Lydia frowned.

"I might need a graphing calculator," she said.

"Why don't we just forget about that?" Johnny

said. "Some of us..." He paused to look down at himself. "...weren't blessed with super speed."

"No joke," Lydia said. "Twelve minutes. That's almost one minute per vampire and probably eleven minutes longer than you've ever had sex."

Johnny was too out of breath to form a retort so he just said, "Fuck you."

"You're the only one who got hurt, too," Gavin pointed out.

"Yes, Gavin, okay, thank you."

The werewolf shrugged. "Should we break off some more fangs?"

"No," Johnny said. "Two is enough."

Gavin frowned. "For what?"

"Dunno," Johnny admitted. "Just a hunch."

Lydia eyed both men, but remained silent.

Johnny put his arms around both of their necks, and they carried him out of the street like an injured football player. Johnny glanced at Lydia.

"Why *are* you so damn fast anyway?"

She shrugged.

"Good genes, I guess."

Johnny tried to put some weight on his bad leg and winced.

"Some Bengay will really help clear that pain up," Lydia said.

Gavin opened his mouth.

"Don't. Gavin, I swear to God, don't say anything," Johnny said.

"I saw some Bengay in your medicine cabinet, at

your apartment," Lydia said.

"You went through my medicine cabinet?" Johnny asked.

"Duh, and yeah, the Bengay was behind the Valtrex."

Johnny gave up, hung his head.

"Fine," he said, "Let's go back. We could probably use some sleep anyways. It's obvious McBride isn't out to kill us. At least not yet."

"Yeah, no," Lydia said, "I'm not staying in that shit hole. I'll probably get herpes."

"Herpes isn't even that bad," Gavin said.

"Okay, no, gross. Leaving now," Lydia said.

"Wait," Johnny said. "Get pictures of the bodies. We'll split the bounty. Maybe split the difference, too?"

"Nope," Lydia said, as she took pictures on her phone.

"Fine," Johnny said.

"Here," Lydia said and held out her phone, "put your number in and we can catch up in the morning."

Gavin and Johnny looked at the phone and then at each other remembering what happened last time. Lydia grinned.

"You 'badass' werewolf bounty hunters are real pussies," she said, and walked away.

Police sirens that had been background noise drew closer.

"Big Bob's," Gavin shouted. "Meet us for

breakfast."

"If you're lucky," Lydia said.

Johnny looked at Gavin.

"Hey, maybe Isabella works mornings too," Gavin said. Then he shouldered the bag of quarters and the bag of weapons, both on one shoulder with no apparent effort. He helped Johnny back upstairs to the shitty apartment.

Johnny didn't want to go back there, but they didn't really have a choice. The inside smelled so bad, the two of them sat out on Johnny's balcony, which creaked under their combined weight. They drank a couple beers and relaxed while they watched the cops shit their pants at the number of corpses lying in the street.

Gavin nodded off first.

"Pussy werewolf," Johnny mumbled. He polished off the beer, put his head against the wall, and closed his eyes for a minute. When he opened them the sun was climbing the sky.

Nudging Gavin with his foot, Johnny winced. His groin hurt more now than the night before.

"Balls," he muttered.

Gavin's eyes opened and he grinned at Johnny.

"Did ya break 'em, Headcase?"

"Damn near. I think we missed breakfast."

"Let's go get lunch then. I'm starving."

Johnny used the railing to lever himself up. It took him a while to stand.

"Yeah," he said. "What else is new?"

# CHAPTER 12

BIG BOB'S was filled with bodies and noise, but the two men saw Lydia at a table by herself and pushed past the line at the door.

She looked up from the enormous pile of bacon on her plate. "Took you long enough."

Helping himself to a handful of bacon, Gavin sat next to her. Johnny lowered himself into the other empty chair. It took a while and the other two watched him while they chewed.

"I'm fine," Johnny said when his butt was on the seat.

"Of course you are," Lydia said.

"Right," Gavin said. "You're Johnny Headcase. You're a legend, man."

Johnny pointed at the bacon and looked at Lydia. She nodded and he took one. For a moment, bacon was chewed and nothing was said. Isabella sidled up to the table and favored Gavin with a friendly smile. He grinned back around the piece of meat on its way into his mouth.

"Everything okay here, guys? Can I get you some coffee or something?"

Lydia shook her head, but Johnny ordered coffee, orange juice, and water.

"Me too, on all three counts," Gavin said. "You work lunches, too, huh?"

Isabella nodded. "Mostly. I hardly ever work nights. I gotta get table nine. I'll bring your drinks back soon."

Watching her walk away, Gavin yelped when Lydia punched him in the kidney.

"Ask her out already."

"I'm gonna. There's a courtship... ritual... thing to be observed."

The pile of bacon got smaller fast as the three shoveled pieces of it in their mouths. Gavin belched loud and long and the other two stared at him as he excused himself. Isabella brought a tray of drinks and, after some heavy eye contact between her and Gavin, everybody sat with their food, drinks and thoughts. Finally, Gavin spoke.

"Lydia, you smell funny."

"Fuck you."

"No. I mean, I don't think you're human," Gavin said.

Lydia mimed a phone to her ear. "Hi, Pot? Yeah, this is the Kettle. Guess what? You're black."

"What are we, twelve?" Johnny asked. "Lydia, you are faster than any human I know. Faster even than me, and I am faster than the werewolf over there. Are you human?"

"You're not faster than me," Gavin said with his mouth full.

"Yes, he is," Lydia said, "You're stronger, but he's definitely faster. Won't last, though—he's getting old."

Johnny shrugged.

"Answer the question."

Instead, Lydia got up and walked to the buffet. She snagged a clean dinner plate and piled it high with sausage links. When she got back, both men ate off her plate and waited. Gavin ate three bites for every one of theirs. After a while, Lydia met Johnny's eyes.

"No. I'm not human. At least, not entirely. Half, definitely."

Johnny sipped his coffee. Gavin swallowed a mouthful of meat and chased it with O.J. Johnny drank more coffee and Gavin tapped his foot.

"Well, what the hell is the other half?" Gavin asked, eventually.

Lydia opened her mouth, but Johnny held up a hand.

"She's on our side. Does it matter?"

Something about Johnny's tone made Gavin sit back and keep his mouth shut. Scowling, he popped another sausage in his mouth and chewed it deliberately. Somehow, only one piece of sausage remained. Lydia tilted the plate toward Johnny, who shook his head. She aimed it at Gavin, who thought about it for several seconds before shrugging. Pulling a billfold from her belt, Lydia peeled off enough to cover all three of them plus a generous tip. It barely made a dent in the roll of money. As the three made their way through the much thinner crowd, Isabella stopped Gavin with a hand on his arm. She handed him a piece of paper.

"You, uh, left this on the table," she stammered. Her cheeks were flushed.

"No, I—" Gavin started, but Lydia elbowed him in the ribs. "Oh. Yeah. Hey, thanks for catching me before I left."

With a girlish smile, Isabella hustled back to the kitchen. Once she was out of sight, they left. Outside in the afternoon sunshine, Gavin opened the note. A phone number and a tiny ink heart were the only things on the paper. Johnny and Lydia leaned in to look and Gavin clutched it to his chest.

"Shut up," he said. He strode away fast. Laughing, Lydia followed. Johnny limped after them.

The trio walked down the cracked sidewalk as commuters flooded the street. Gavin and Lydia led the way and Johnny hobbled behind them. Every so often they glanced back, but they took almost three strides to Johnny's one. They laughed and leaned in and whispered and Johnny felt sweat from both the heat of the day and embarrassment trickle down his face and darken his armpits.

Some kid riding a bicycle with a sack of

newspapers slung over his shoulder almost ran Johnny down.

"Hey, watch it you little prick," Johnny yelled.

The bike's tires screeched as the kid skidded to a stop. Johnny looked forward. Gavin and Lydia were probably two hundred yards ahead of him.

"You're walking in the bike lane," the kid said, pedaling up.

"Bike lane? On the sidewalk? This is America, kid."

"Look down, asshole."

Johnny did, and sure enough his legs straddled a painted yellow line he'd never noticed before.

"I don't, I didn't know..." Johnny stammered. "Fucking hippies."

"Well, now you do," the kid said. The kid pulled a rolled up newspaper out of his pack and slapped Johnny across the face with it. "Make sure you don't forget it, pops."

Too flabbergasted to react, Johnny's mouth fell open and he just blinked at the kid.

"You're not saying sorry, sweaty?" the kid said. "Old people got no respect." He rode away.

After finally finding his breath, Johnny yelled, "Sorry," at the kid's back.

The paperboy slammed his bike brakes again, spun it around, and pulled a paper out of his bag.

"Thank you. Was that so hard?"

Johnny shook his head.

"Special delivery. On the house, asshole," the kid

said and wound up. He threw the newspaper like a fastball at Johnny's face. And promptly fell off his bike when Johnny shot a hand up and caught the paper a few inches from impact. The kid scrambled to get back on his bike.

Johnny cocked the paper to throw it back. He knew he could impale the little shit. A hand grabbed the paper and the paperboy rode away without looking back.

"Easy, tiger," Gavin said.

"Did you just get beat up by the paperboy?" Lydia asked.

Johnny squeezed his eyes shut. He rubbed the bridge of his nose.

"Okay, first of all, he was, like, twelve. I'm not gonna fight a prepubescent. Plus, my groin hurts. And the little turd started it. He almost ran me over."

"Well, you were walking in the bike lane," Lydia said.

Before Johnny could answer her Gavin said, "So you admit you got beat up by the paperboy."

"Yeah, well I was about to bean him when you grabbed my hand," Johnny said.

"And give up a free newspaper?" Gavin *tsked* his tongue and shook his head. "Give me that."

Johnny handed him the newspaper, and Gavin swatted him on the back of the head with it.

"Well, thanks for coming back to check on me," Johnny said with some ice in his voice. "I thought you'd forgotten about me."

"We were discussing what to do with you," Gavin said. "Clearly you can't keep up."

"He also asked me about a hundred times what I thought he should do about Isabella," Lydia said.

Now it was Gavin's turn to turn red.

"So what are you going to do with me? Put me down? Send me to the glue factory?"

"We thought about it." Lydia smirked.

Behind her Gavin jabbed a finger at Lydia and mouthed, "all her idea."

Johnny laughed.

She turned and Gavin had his face buried in the newspaper.

"So what did you decide?"

"Well, I know somebody; I guess you could call her a holistic healer," she said. "But she's on the other side of town. And she's a bit… eccentric."

"Great, at this rate we'll get there by Thursday."

"We got that figured out too, don't we Gavin?"

Gavin didn't answer.

Lydia ignored him and kept talking.

"We can't take a cab in this traffic, so right before you got your ass kicked by One Direction a minute ago, we were going to head into that pharmacy and rent you a wheelchair. We figured by the time we picked one out, paid for it, and took a nap, you'd probably be near the front door." She pointed to a corner store a few hundred yards away.

"Great," Johnny said.

"It's the only way," Lydia said. "Right, Gavin?"

He didn't answer. He was still engrossed in the newspaper.

Lydia snapped the paper with her finger, "Hello, earth to Gavin."

"Yeah, go ahead, I'll catch up," he muttered, not looking up.

"Jesus Christ," Lydia said. "Fine."

Johnny took a pathetic, hobbling step and Lydia looked at Gavin, then threw her hands up in the air.

"Fucking grade A gentleman," she said under her breath.

Then she ducked down, grunted, and threw Johnny over her shoulder. She probably expected him to fight or protest, but he just accepted it.

"Your hair smells good," Johnny said, head bobbing over her shoulder.

"You're all sweaty, fucking ewwww," Lydia said.

She was strong but the walk was slow and a little awkward. They received lots of weird looks from other pedestrians. Johnny grinned and waved at a few of them, even pointed at her ass and winked and gave a thumbs up. A few paces from the drug store Lydia paused.

"Is that your… Are you fucking hard right now?"

Johnny shrugged.

"You smell fantastic and I'm staring straight at your ass. It's a nice one. And I'm kind of rubbing against your boob. Take it as a compliment."

"I can't…" she didn't finish. She threw Johnny to

the pavement like a sack of concrete. "Wait here and pray I don't buy something in there to kill you with."

"Awwww, I'm not your type?"

She blew air into her bangs.

"Don't fucking push me, Headcase."

"That's not a 'no'."

She went inside the pharmacy while he dragged himself to the edge of the building and slumped up against it.

Lydia came out a few minutes later pushing an empty wheelchair with a brown paper sack on it.

"I got you an extra present," she said helping him into the chair.

He opened the package.

"Here, Stinky. Deodorant with extra antiperspirant. If anyone needs it, it's you."

"Thanks," he said.

Gavin trotted up with a weird look on his face.

"Finally," Lydia said. "What the hell is your problem? I'm all wet because of you."

Gavin and Johnny exchanged looks.

"Sweat. Fucking sweat okay? God, I swear. What happened to you anyway?"

"First, is it—"

"Yes," Lydia interrupted. "Yes, it is way too early to even think about calling Isabella. Now, what's second?"

"Sorry," Gavin said, and flipped the newspaper around, "You guys have to see this."

Johnny started to stand, but Lydia shoved him back in the chair. She took the paper from Gavin and held it so Johnny could read, too. Grinning out at them with that Hollywood smile, McBride stood above the headline: Local Billionaire Philanthropist to Open Hospital and Blood Bank. Lydia snorted.

"Blood bank? Seriously?"

"Guy's got a lot of balls," Johnny said.

"Yeah, but I bet his are still in one piece," Gavin said.

"You're gonna want to back off givin' me shit, Wolf," Johnny said. "I'm on the verge of losing my temper."

"What are you gonna do from the wheelchair, roll over my toes? Shit, Headcase, right now you're about as scary as my grandma."

Johnny's gun was a blur. The loud report, muzzle flash and the small round hole in Gavin's forehead happened all at once. Blood and brains splattered the concrete pole behind Gavin. He fell on his ass and, moments later, toppled to one side.

# HEADCASE

## COLDBLOODED HOT DEMONS

Look for Part 2

Coming September 2020

# GROWING UP:

# JOHNNY'S STORY

Johnny was at his best on the mound. Out there alone, cap shading his eyes, he stood like a king, or a god maybe.

He eyed the batter: Kevin Donal. A lefty. Kid could hit, too. Last season, he put three over the right field fence.

Kevin Donal also put the moves on Johnny's girl. Sure, all they had done was made out a few times, but they were going steady, dammit! And, nobody, especially not no left-handed slugger *chump* was going to get the better of Johnny Armstrong.

He screwed the ball into the leather of his glove, warming it up. He whispered to it, telling it what he wanted to do, like that Tigers pitcher, Fidrych. The Bird, they called him. Said he was crazy. Said he pulled down his pants on the mound, because he forgot his jock. Crazy or not, the man could pitch.

Now, living in Queen City, Johnny was a Sharks fan, like every other kid in town. But, when they played Detroit, well, it was awful hard to root against the best pitcher in the league. Best in the game.

When he finished talking to the ball, Johnny threw it. A picture-perfect inside fastball, and Kevin Donal went for it.

At the last possible second, the ball dipped, sliding under the bat, and *smack!* into the catcher's glove.

One ball and two strikes later, and the Donal kid walked away with nothing but a bruised ego. Which was just what was gonna happen with Sheila.

Johnny let a couple guys get on base that game, but none of them scored. And, every single time Kevin Donal came up to the plate, Johnny struck him out, always throwing hard, always throwing inside.

The last time, in the eighth inning, Johnny launched a fastball up and in and Kevin took a hack at it but it was impossible to tell if he thought he could hit it or it was just self-defense.

Kevin spat, screamed, and stormed the mound, dragging his Louisville Slugger in the dirt behind him, leaving a trail like a lizard's tail.

Johnny took off his glove and dropped it next to him. He wiped his hands on his white uniform pants and waited. Being on the mound made him seem even taller than he was, and he was already big for thirteen.

Donal came right up, snarling, and poked him in the chest with the business end of the bat. "You're doing it on purpose. Up here throwing junk. Sending me pitches I can't hit. Admit it."

Johnny shrugged. "Shit, man, I didn't tell you to swing at any of those. And what if I am? That is the object of baseball."

"It's cheating. That's what." He poked Johnny a little harder with the bat.

"You're gonna wanna stop that now."

Donal sneered. "Stop what? This." He poked Johnny again.

Johnny snatched the bat from him with one hand. Splinters flew as he broke the hardwood over his knee masking the pain with a vicious smile. Pointing the jagged end at Donal, he said, "Back off. You lost fair and square. Suck it up, buttercup. Now get off my mound."

Donal smacked the half-bat aside and swung a left hook at Johnny's face.

Johnny took it, rolled with it, minimizing the damage. He dropped the bat pieces and laid into the kid. Both fists hitting over and over: body blows, clips to the face.

Donal put his hands up, but Johnny was too fast. His hands found the holes in the other boy's defenses and his fists hammered home.

The Little League coach ran up to the mound yelling his head off, but Johnny only heard noise; he couldn't make out words.

Donal looked at the coach, dropping his guard for a half-second.

J o h n n y  t a g g e d  h i m  f u l l - f o r c e, rattling Donal's teeth and putting his lights out.

"Damn it, Armstrong! What are you thinking? This is *baseball*, not the boxing ring. You're out!"

"What the hell, Coach? He came at me and I defended myself and you're gonna bench me now?"

"Don't talk back to me, boy. You're out. You're off the team. You're out of Little League. You'll never play in this town again."

Johnny stared at the man. Up on the mound, he was the same height. "You're kicking me out of baseball?"

"Yeah. You're a damn hooligan, Johnny."

"He came at me, and I defended myself. What am I missing here?"

"Look at him! He doesn't have a nose anymore."

Johnny shrugged and held his ground.

"What you gonna do, hit me too?" The coach sneered. "I don't go down as easy as a kid, Johnny."

Johnny hit him on the cheekbone with a left, then dropped into a crouch, ducking the man's clumsy swing. He came up hard with an uppercut. His whole body was behind it.

The coach fell on his butt, stunned.

"Baseball's my life," Johnny told him.

The coach spat out a tooth around his unhinged jaw. "Not anymore."

Johnny turned in a slow circle, looking at each of his teammates, coaches, opponents and fans in the crowd. Every one of them avoided his eyes as they inspected the grass, whispered to each other or pretended to stare at the horizon.

Johnny walked to the dugout and grabbed his bag and headed home without another word.

It wasn't until he reached his front door that the pain kicked in. He looked down at his hands. His knuckles were busted open and though the blood had dried, it left some nasty smears on his white baseball pants. Some drips landed all the way down on his cleats. He could barely move his fingers or his wrists. Nothing felt broken, but he didn't doubt severe sprains and then some in both hands. But none of that hurt as much as getting booted from the team by that smug coach, who'd never had his back.

He'd been pitching a solid game! So what if he threw a lot of pitches high and inside? He never hit a person, never even got warned by an umpire. And now that fucking Donal took something else from him. While his coach, of all people, sided with Donal.

Unbelievable.

Thinking about all this brought the rage back all over again and he forgot about the pain. All Johnny wanted to do was break shit or hurt someone. He tried breathing deep, tried counting to ten, tried pacing through the kitchen, but he couldn't bring himself to see anything but red.

With the words of his coach echoing in his head, Johnny forgot all about the pain in his wrists and fists. He went to the basement and took it all out on the heavy bag. Sweat poured down his face, his lungs burned, and his fists throbbed, but he kept going until he nearly collapsed from exhaustion and a desperate need for water.

Johnny left the bag swinging and turned to head up the stairs, but let out a gasp when he saw his father sitting on them, waiting, with a bottle of water in one hand and two bags of frozen peas on the step beside him.

"Let me see," his father said.

Johnny chewed his lip a moment before he held out both his bloody, swollen hands. The bruises had settled in looking like black and blue camouflage. His father shook his head.

"Jesus Christ. Kid, the only thing bigger than your temper might be your tolerance for pain."

Johnny looked down, didn't meet his father's eyes.

"Maybe my hatred for injustice," Johnny muttered.

"We'll talk about it. Do we need to go to the hospital?"

Johnny shook his head.

"Okay, go ice your hands while I make us some dinner."

Johnny realized how hungry he was when he smelled the ground beef sizzling in the skillet. He'd tried to help his father cook, but his father refused, which Johnny secretly appreciated because he didn't know if he'd even be able to feed himself. His hands felt ruined.

"Your coach called me at work."

"I'm surprised he could talk."

His father smacked his fist on the table. Johnny jolted.

"This is not funny, kid. It was your other coach. The one you clocked is going to be on an all-milkshake diet for at least six months. I'm trying to finish up my day at work, feeling bad enough already that I'm missing your game and then guess what? Out of nowhere, I get a flustered call from a coach saying that you beat up a player on the other team, broke a bat over your knee and punched out your own coach. What in the blue hell happened out there?"

Johnny sighed.

"I was pitching, throwing a pretty good game, and Kevin Donal comes up for the fourth time. I'd struck him out three times already and I got him to take a wild swing at a high inside fastball."

His father held up a hand to silence him.

"How high and inside?"

"C'mon, Dad, if I wanted to hit him in the head, we both know that's what I would've done. I was just looking to humble him. Anyway, he swung and missed and charged the mound with his bat. Poked it into my chest and started with the threats, so I snatched the bat from him, and broke it over my knee. I thought that'd be enough, but I was wrong. He threw a punch, so I took it, and then I beat the shit out of him. Coach comes over to break it up, tells me I'm out of control and not only benches me, but kicks me off the team right there on the mound. He called me a hooligan, and I guess I proved him right."

"Jesus, kid," his father said and patted him on the shoulder. "I'm not mad; I can't be. Not at you defending yourself and standing your ground. But it's bad, Johnny, real bad. They're talking about suspending or expelling you from school, maybe even pressing charges."

"I didn't do anything wrong."

"Maybe you didn't, kid, but that doesn't really matter, does it? It's your word against theirs and those coaches carry a lot more credibility than a loose cannon thirteen-year-old your size. The world is full of injustice, and this is the kind of shit you can step in if you don't control that temper."

"You can't be blaming me for this, you just can't," Johnny fumed.

"I'm not, Johnny. But you've got to be aware that, in the real world, doing the right thing, standing up for yourself, or even defending yourself can have dire, life-altering consequences. You've got to pick your spots and realize that the hill you're defending may not always be worth dying on, even if it isn't your fault."

Johnny opened his mouth.

"No," his father said. "No more. Don't argue with me. Just think about it. Think about no more baseball, possibly no more school, and the pain that's flaring through both your hands. This isn't a punishment, but a lesson about actions and consequences. I need you to think hard and soak it all in, and if we need to talk more tomorrow or whenever, we will. For now, eat."

Johnny struggled to feed himself, but declined help when his father offered. After dinner his father gave him a half-dozen ibuprofen. Johnny swallowed them.

"Now head on upstairs and take a nice long shower, ice those wrists again afterward and get a good night's sleep. Tomorrow might really suck."

Johnny nodded.

"Thanks, Dad."

His father smiled, and hugged him.

Johnny walked to the bathroom on leaden feet.

After a couple weeks, Johnny's hands and wrists were pretty much healed. He'd kept them wrapped for the first couple days, but after that was able to use them, though stiff and clumsy.

He tried not to dwell on the fact that he couldn't play ball, but of course he did. He wrote a letter to the coach, apologizing for hitting him. He got one in return that said the coach appreciated the apology, but that it changed nothing.

What did that leave him? His grades were okay. He wasn't dumb, and usually wasn't lazy. He just didn't care that much about the War of 1812, or how to conjugate verbs in French. All he wanted to do was pitch for the Majors.

To make matters worse, when Sheila heard about what happened on the pitcher's mound, she refused to speak to Johnny.

No baseball.

No girlfriend.

"No point," he said aloud.

"What's that?"

"Nothing, Dad. Just grumbling about the whole thing, you know?"

His father gave him a long, considering look. "Yeah. I get that."

Johnny studied his dad: the scar tissue around his eyes, the broken nose, and the big, swollen knuckles. He had been a heavyweight contender, but never quite good enough to make a run for the title fights.

"What?"

Johnny shrugged. "Maybe I could box."

His dad put his coffee cup down. "It's a hard life, kid."

"I know."

"I'm not gonna tell you 'no.' I mean, you've got a solid foundation already."

"Thanks to you."

His dad smiled. "Well, yeah. Had to teach my kid how to defend himself. What kind of father would I be otherwise?"

"So?"

"All right. We'll go to the gym Saturday. I'll set

you up with Vinny. He'll give you the basics. If you have an aptitude for it, we'll find someone to push you beyond that."

Since Johnny had already learned the basics from his own dad, Vinny covered the rest. He focused on footwork and defense, since those were Johnny's weaknesses. In a few months, Vinny called Johnny's dad over. "Kid's a natural. Picks it up fast. He's ready to spar with a welterweight, I think."

"Hold off on that for a while, Vin. I'm not even sure I want him to box, you know? Sport hasn't really done me any favors."

"You were good, man."

"Not good enough."

"Whatever. Not gonna argue with you. If not this, then what's the kid gonna do?"

"I was thinking bail bonds. Like you."

Vinny watched Johnny lay into the speed bag. His fists were almost a blur. At only thirteen, this kid was already looking formidable. "It can get dangerous."

"Yeah."

"Pays good though."

"Yeah."

"It were my kid? I'd say no. But, it ain't my kid."

"Yeah."

"You want me to show him the ropes, I'll do it."

"Do it."

"So, how's this work?"

Vinny looked at him. "Pretty simple, really. We get the bad guys, and bring 'em back to jail."

"Sounds easy enough."

Vinny smiled. "Can be. Sometimes, though, they don't wanna go."

"Makes sense, I guess."

"Right. Sure. But, that's when it gets complicated. No gloves out here, chief. This is the real world."

"Okay. So, you got any 'real-world' advice on gettin' the bad guys?"

Vinny nodded thoughtfully. "You hit the soft parts of their bodies with the hard parts of yours. And, you hit the hard parts of their bodies with something else."

"Vinny?"

"Yeah, kid?"

"That's the best advice I've ever heard."

"Thanks."

Their 'client,' a cowboy with a metal briefcase, stepped out of the motel room door.

Vinny nudged Johnny and they crossed the lot toward him.

He almost had the key in the door when Johnny called out. "Marty!"

The cowboy turned, looking puzzled. "I know you, kid?"

Johnny shook his head. "Not yet. I'm a big fan though."

"What?"

Johnny kicked him in the nuts, hard.

With a whoosh of air, the cowboy collapsed forward, losing his grip on the briefcase.

Johnny grabbed it off the pavement, and hit the cowboy in the head three times.

The guy was out. Blood trickled from his nose and dribbled toward the storm drain.

Vinny slow-clapped. "Yup. That's the way to do it."

"Hey, just following the hard part/soft part advice. Told you it was good. Went a lot better than my last fight, which was all fist against skull."

"Sometimes that's unavoidable," Vinny said squatting down. "Help me roll this fat ass over."

Johnny helped Vinny flip the cowboy onto his belly and cuffed his hands behind his back.

"You only made one mistake," Vinny said, "but it's a big one."

Johnny's eyes flicked from the cowboy to Vinny where they lingered, looking for some kind of hint.

"Got me stumped," Johnny said.

"Unless it's life and death, don't ever knock out anyone over three hundred pounds. This is gonna suck," Vinny said kicking Marty in the ass.

"Can't we just... you know, use that smelly stuff they use to wake people up on TV? Don't you have that?"

Vinny laughed and shook his head.

"The way you're built and the way you move and

fight Johnny, sometimes it's hard to remember you're barely a teenager. He didn't lose consciousness at the sight of blood, you scrambled his brains with that briefcase. Hell, he might be in a coma."

Johnny made a face.

"Don't sweat it, kid. You don't do that and he gets a chance to pull a weapon on you, it could end a whole lot worse."

To prove his point, Vinny frisked the body, removing two guns and a knife. A shoulder holster, ankle holster and belt sheath.

Johnny's stomach twisted when he saw the weapons and realized how easily things could've gone sideways.

"So, you just turned me loose on this guy armed to the teeth?" Johnny said, his face reddening, temper threatening to flare.

Vinny shrugged.

"I was pretty sure you'd be fine, and I was right."

Johnny's lips curled into an angry sneer and his fists balled up.

"Jesus, kid, your dad wasn't kidding. Look, don't get mad at me because I trained you well and sort of had full confidence in you. And if it went off the rails, I had your back, even if it didn't look like it. Trust me. Okay?"

Johnny said nothing. Didn't blink.

"I'm gonna get the car, so we don't have to carry this fat fuck across the parking lot. While I'm gone, take a breath and cool off. We won. Everything's fine."

Vinny turned his back and took a step toward the car.

Johnny's fists clenched, but instead of pouncing, he heeded Vinny's advice again. Johnny closed his eyes, took a few breaths and composed himself. Not long ago his father had given him some solid advice about choice and consequence. Vinny'd done the same before taking down the cowboy.

The car pulled up and the window rolled down.

"We good?"

Johnny nodded.

"Okay then, open the back door."

Johnny obliged and even with their combined strength, getting the overweight, deadweight cowboy into the backseat was the hardest part of the day. Vinny was right again.

Johnny walked over and picked up the briefcase, which now looked like a flattened Coke can.

"Good god, kid, you sure did a number on his head with that case. Hope they don't need anything in there for evidence, I don't think Houdini could get that open."

"Like you said, use something else for the hard parts."

"Just gotta make sure the bulk of the damage stays on the weapon. If his head looked like this thing, we'd have some explaining to do. Remember, we're bail bondsman, not hitmen. It sort of works the opposite way."

"Noted," Johnny said, walking around to the passenger side.

"You're really something, kid," Vinny said.

He looked at Johnny, looked at the cowboy, looked at the battered briefcase, and smirked.

"A real fucking headcase. I can't wait to tell your dad."

# ABOUT THE AUTHORS

KEN MACGREGOR'S work has appeared in dozens of anthologies and magazines, and the occasional podcast. He has two story collections: *An Aberrant Mind*, and *Sex, Gore & Millipedes*, a middle-grade novella: *Devil's Bane*, and is a member of the Great Lakes Association of Horror Writers (GLAHW). He has also written TV commercials, sketch comedy, a music video, and a zombie movie. He is the Managing Editor of Collections/Anthologies for LVP Publications, and curated an anthology (*Burnt Fur*) for Blood Bound Books. When not writing, Ken drives the bookmobile for his local library. He lives with his kids, two cats, and the ashes of his wife. Ken can be found at ken-macgregor.com.

KERRY LIPP is the author of several short stories that have been featured in many anthologies and podcasts. A few years ago he fell off the face of the earth, but he comes back to visit every now and then. Headcase is his first novel.